Let's Play BASKETBALL!

Charles R. Smith Jr.
illustrated by Terry Widener

CANDLEWICK PRESS
CAMBRIDGE, MASSACHUSETTS

I'm bored. . . . Take me out to play!

*It's me, your **BASKETBALL**.*
*Let's have some **FUN** today!*

We could **BOUNCE** *to the park,*

DRIBBLE to a funky beat.

SPIN with me,

DANCE *with me on concrete!*

HOLD me,

FLICK me . . .

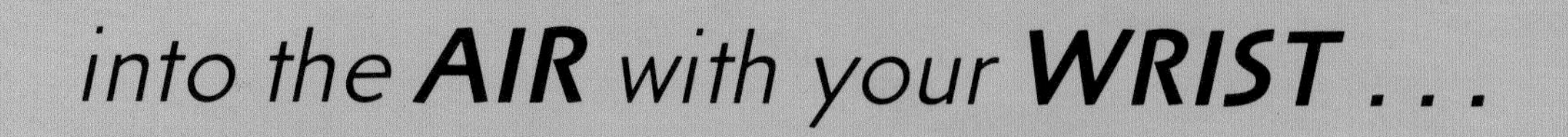

into the ***AIR*** *with your* ***WRIST . . .***

over the ***BACKBOARD.***

Watch me **GO-GO-GO. . . .**

See me **TWIST** and **TWIST** and **TWIST**! . . .

I'll TURN

and SKIP

and LEAP

and **RISE**

as I **BOUNCE** off the sun

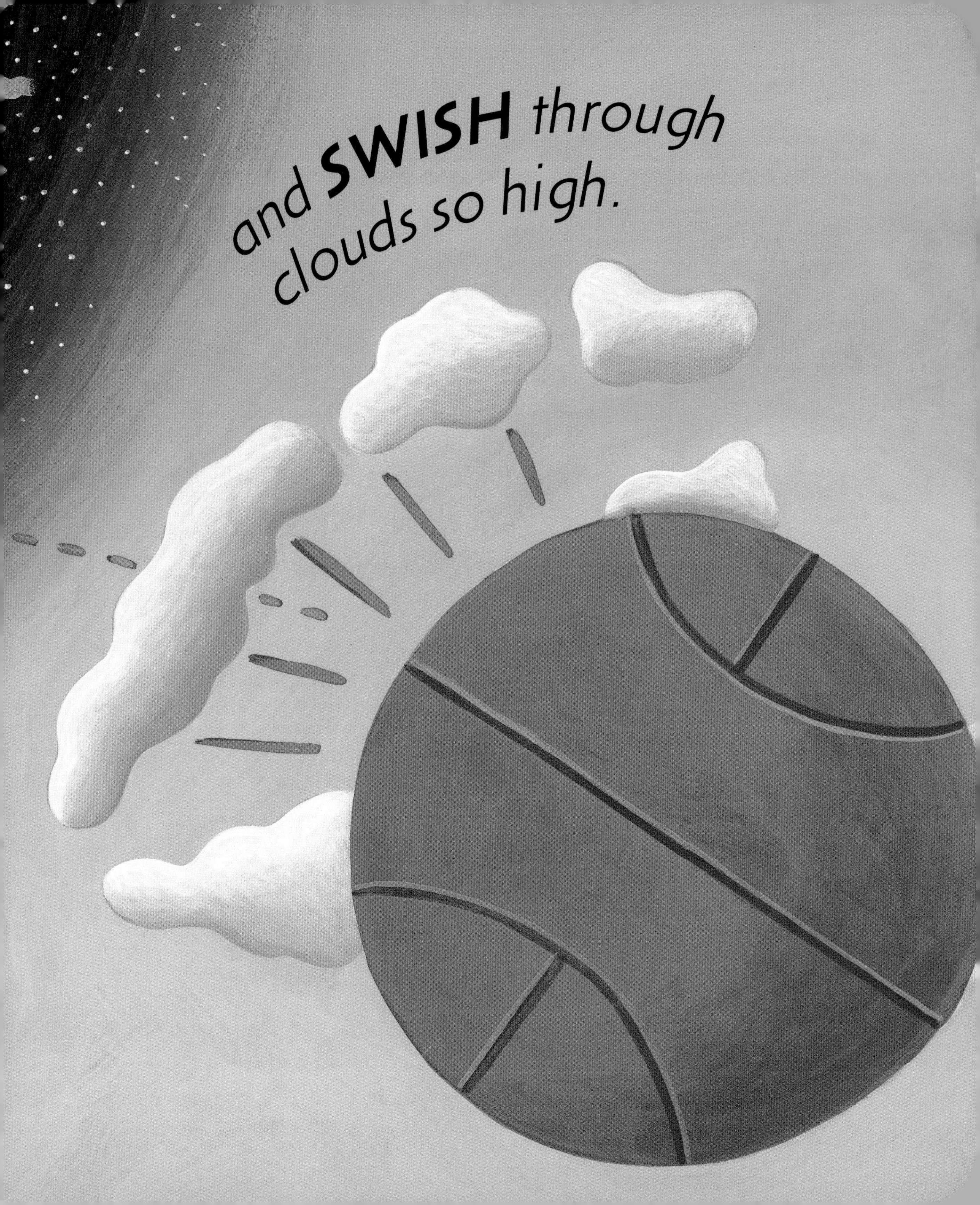

and **SWISH** *through*
clouds so high.

If you'll **PLEASE,**
PLEASE,
PLEASE . . .